CHOOSE YOUR OWN ADVENTURER

ALI HOUSE

Published in Canada by Engen Books, St. John's, NL.

ISBN: 978-1-989473-23-8

Distributed by:
Engen Books
www.engenbooks.com
submissions@engenbooks.com

First mass market paperback printing: September 2019

Cover Design: Ali House

CHOOSE YOUR OWN ADVENTURER

CAMPAIGN 1
ORIGIN STORY

TABLE OF CONTENTS

THE THIRSTY THISTLE

The town of Quarryville was unusually quiet for early afternoon. Stores had been shuttered and closed up, and homes were quiet and uninviting. As Aeris wandered through the empty streets, she wondered where everyone was. Whenever she travelled to a new town, she normally received strange looks from the townspeople – suspicious looks usually reserved for an outsider who didn't belong – but here there was nobody around to pay her any attention.

Given the history of this town, it was possible that they were all hiding inside their homes, cowering in fear, waiting for danger to pass. Aeris couldn't help feeling sorry for these poor villagers. A life spent in fear was not a good life, and these people had been living under a tyrant's reign for far too long. As she walked, a sense of duty and determination welled up inside of her, and each step along these vacant streets strengthened her resolve to help the people of this town. They needed a hero and here she was.

As there was nobody around to talk with, she headed for the local tavern. Experience told her that a tavern was always a good place to go when arriving in an unfamiliar town for the first time. No matter what strange habits the townsfolk might have, you could always depend on the fact that at least one of them would be quenching their thirst with a mug of ale.

Upon spotting a sign declaring 'The Thirsty Thistle', Aeris took in a deep breath, squared her shoulders, and headed inside. It looked exactly like every other tavern she'd ever been in, from the well-worn wooden tables and chairs placed on the dirt-covered floor, to the soot-covered fireplaces against every wall. It was quieter than she'd expected, despite being half-full of patrons. Some sat alone, while others sat in groups two or three, but they were all silent as they drank from tarnished mugs.

She confidently strode over to the barkeep, aware of how out of place she must look with her white armour, which had been polished to a shine, and her clean olive skin. Her long blond hair had been tied back with a leather cord, and her blue eyes were bright and eager. The other patrons wore outfits of leather or cloth, coloured in browns and greens, and were looking at her with frowns upon their dirt-streaked faces. Despite this discomfort, she resolved to be unshakable in spirit.

"Greetings. I am Aeris Greatsoul and I am here to speak with the mayor of this village."

The barkeep gave her the once-over with her

narrow green eyes, an amused smile on her dark-skinned face. "Here to slay a dragon, are you?"

"Not particularly," Aeris replied, surprised by the teasing tone. She squared her shoulders again and smiled, reinforcing her aura of politeness and authority. "However, I am here to speak to the mayor nonetheless."

"Have an appointment then, do you?"

"No, but it is very important that we speak."

The barkeep smirked and nodded. "He's on your left, green hat," she replied, holding back a laugh.

Aeris politely thanked her for the information before quickly turning away. Holding her head high, she walked over to the man with the green hat. He was a lean man with brown skin, wearing dark brown pants and a green vest, both of which showed signs of having been mended multiple times. He was sitting by himself, one hand wrapped around a mug, the fingers of the other hand tapping lightly on the wooden tabletop as he stared off into space.

"Mayor?"

He startled and looked up at her, squinting. "Do I know you?"

"Not yet. My name is Aeris Greatsoul and I am here to help you in your fight against the evil warlock Grimgrax."

She paused for dramatic effect, but instead of the jubilant cheer or wide-eyed awe she'd been expecting, the mayor looked confused.

"Why?" he asked.

"Um... Because he is taking money from your village in return for 'protection', and that's wrong."

The mayor shrugged. "Honestly, we're okay with

it."

Aeris' mouth dropped open. She couldn't have heard him right. "Excuse me?"

"I mean, we could definitely use the money, don't get me wrong. A few buildings need repairs, and medicine is hard to come by, and it'd be nice to build up a trade with other towns, but we have enough to get by. Whenever we find ourselves running short of food we turn to the Karloff family, who are excellent hunters, and the Springdoves really know how to forage. Besides, it's easier to give Grimgrax all that money instead of having him burn our village down. It's much more cost-effective."

"But... But it's wrong."

He shrugged again. "There are a lot of things in life that aren't right, but that's why us humans are built to adapt, eh?"

The mayor took a long drink from his mug and Aeris had a feeling that their conversation had come to an end. She didn't understand what was going on. She'd expected the mayor to be delighted by her offer to help, not to refuse it. What was she to do now? Should she respect the mayor's wishes and leave? Should she fight the warlock anyway? Deflated, she started to walk away, but she didn't get far before a frantic red-headed young woman raced into the tavern.

"Mayor Minemax! Mayor Minemax!" she shouted, rushing over to his table. "Our tithe has disappeared! It was in your office, counted and ready to go, and I only turned my back for a second, but when I looked again it was gone!"

The blood drained from the mayor's face. "Are you certain, Adelia?"

She nodded furiously, her brown eyes filled with concern and her pale face creased with worry. "I'm so sorry, Mayor Minemax."

A smile started to cross Aeris' face, which she quickly put an end to. Playing it cool, she replaced it with a neutral expression and looked back at the mayor. He turned to her, his smile gone and his eyes pleading.

"So... that offer about helping us... does it still stand...?"

She nodded pleasantly and placed her right fist over her heart. "A paladin's offer never expires."

"Great!" The mayor jumped to his feet, almost knocking over the table in his haste. "Grimgrax will be here soon, in a clearing in the centre of town. Please take care of him before he can burn anything down." The mayor gave her a terrified smile and raced out of the bar, the young woman scampering behind him.

Aeris took in a deep breath and strode towards the door. She wanted to go to the centre of town right away and get the lay of the land before the warlock arrived. It was always a good idea to scout out any natural advantages that might exist, especially when fighting on unfamiliar territory.

"Hey! Paladin!"

She turned around to see a broad young man with brown skin and brown hair weaving through the tables, walking towards her with a determined look on his face. He was wearing brown leather armour and had a large axe resting on his shoulder. There was nothing familiar about him, so she was unsure why he had called out to her.

"Yes?" she inquired politely.

"Did I hear the mayor say that you could fight the warlock?" he demanded as he drew close.

"Yes. The tithe has gone missing, so–"

"Don't bother," he interrupted. "I came here with the intent of killing Grimgrax, so you can forget about it and go home. I'll handle this."

She was taken aback by his frankness. "And who exactly are you?"

"I am Grendel Longfield, the man who will put an end to that terrible warlock once and for all."

"I will not back down," Aeris said proudly. "I swore an oath that I would stop him, and stop him I shall."

The man frowned, narrowing his brown eyes. "I refuse to let myself be sidelined by a *paladin*." He said the last word as if it tasted disgusting in his mouth.

"And just what do you have against paladins?" She was finding it difficult to maintain her serenity around this stranger and his open hostility. Although she was half a foot taller than him, he managed to appear like he was looking down his nose at her.

He scowled. "They get it into their thick heads that they can solve every problem in the world, and refuse to stay out of other people's ways." With those words, he turned away from her and strode towards the exit.

She hurried after him. "I cannot stay out of your way because this quest is not entirely mine. I am doing this on the behalf of many other people, all of whom are depending on me to succeed."

He ignored her and exited the tavern, heading towards the middle of town. Aeris followed him closely. Maybe once they arrived at the clearing she'd be able to talk him out of this fool's errand. Although she knew nothing about this young man, he'd have to listen to reason. She was a paladin, after all, and he was merely a young man with an axe. They seemed to be similar in age, but he had none of the training that she'd gone through, so it would be best for him to leave this kind of work to her, lest Grimgrax succeed through his inexperience.

As they walked in silence, she built up a compelling and heart-felt case of why he should leave the task to her, barely taking note of the small houses or greenery they passed along the way.

"What is this?" Grendel groaned, coming to a sudden stop.

Snapping out of her thoughts, Aeris stopped short and noticed that they'd arrived at the clearing. It was a large meadow with trees surrounding it, and standing near the centre was a young blonde man, tall and thin with pale skin, wearing dark blue robes. He was holding a large leather-bound book, flipping through the pages at a frantic pace.

Although Aeris had never seen Grimgrax before, she knew that this couldn't be him. Grimgrax was older, wore robes of black and red, and had a reputation for being extremely intimidating. Even if that was all an illusion, she doubted that the evil warlock would ever risk letting anyone see him so unprepared.

"May I help you?" she asked, striding up to the stranger.

He was so started by her words that he almost dropped his book. "Oh, no, sorry, just trying to work out my strategy."

"Strategy for what?" Grendel demanded, coming

up beside Aeris.

"Oh, um, well, my name is Corin Avensound and I am here to stop the evil warlock Grimgrax and end his reign of terror." He looked very pleased with himself, despite the shaky start.

Aeris felt a large sigh building up inside of her and fought the impulse to put her head in her hands.

"Get in line..." Grendel muttered. "Preferably after this one," he hooked a thumb towards Aeris.

Corin looked confused. "What's going on?"

"It turns out that we are also here to stop Grimgrax," Aeris said helpfully. "The mayor was initially against this idea, but after the tithe was stolen he gave me permission to fight on his behalf. As I am certain that neither of you have this permission, I suggest that you stand aside and let me handle this."

"But I can't!" he exclaimed. "I have a mission! I can't stand by and let someone else do something so important to me!"

"Yes, you can," Grendel said. "And I'm not suggesting that you stand in the sidelines, I'm *telling* you to. Let me handle this."

"No, let me handle this," Aeris spoke up.

"The paladin doesn't speak for me, and neither do you, kid. Back off or I'll be forced to make you two back off."

The others frowned at Grendel's words and soon the three of them were arguing about who most deserved to do the deed and why the others needed to go away, all without listening to a single word that anyone else said.

"My, my, Adelia, how you've changed..."

The trio went deathly silent and all at once they

turned in the direction of the new voice. About ten feet away was a tall man with pale skin and long black hair, wearing robes as dark as night. In one hand he held a black staff which emitted a red glow, even in the bright daylight. His eyes, which were also red, burned with impatience. The evil warlock had arrived.

"Where is Adelia with the tithe?" Grimgrax asked, his voice as sharp as a dagger.

Aeris cleared her throat, but before she could reply Grendel let out a roar and charged forward, his axe held high. Before he could make it half-way to his target, Grimgrax raised his hand and fired a bolt of dark, crackling energy, hitting Grendel square in the chest. Aeris jumped out of the way as Grendel was propelled backwards, but Corin was not so lucky. Grendel slammed into him, knocking them both to the ground.

Aeris raced towards the warlock, her sword ready and her shield raised to block any attack that might be coming. He sent another bolt of energy, but she dodged it, not losing any momentum. When she was close enough, she raised her sword high.

"You shall pay for your crimes against the innocent!" she yelled as she brought the sword down.

Grimgrax blocked her attack with his staff. It was obviously infused with strong magic since it held her blade instead of being sliced in two. This close, Aeris could see that it was made of dark wood with a twisted claw at the top. There were veins carved around the staff, revealing a glowing red core. It made sense that his staff would look as evil as he was.

Aeris was surprised by his strength and felt her own start to falter as he pressed her. As her sword started to move back towards her, she thought of all the people she'd sworn to help and prayed to Arete for the strength to win. However, before she could finish her prayer, she felt a shift in the weight of the staff. Moving to her right to compensate, she was suddenly hit square in the back with an electrical charge that coursed throughout her body. Grimacing in pain, she could faintly hear Corin's terrified apology as she felt to the ground, contorting with residual energy.

Grimgrax laughed as he fired a blast of energy at Corin, hitting the distracted wizard in the chest, sending him and his book to the ground again. Still smiling, the warlock looked down at Aeris, who was trying unsuccessfully to gain control of her body. He raised his hand towards her.

"Lord Grimgrax! Lord Grimgrax!" a familiar voice called out. Aeris turned and saw the red-headed woman from the tavern hurrying towards the scene. "Mayor Minemax and I apologize for our lateness! We had the tithe ready this morning, but it has been stolen from us by some unknown scoundrel!"

The warlock lowered his hand and turned to her. "Is this true, Adelia?"

She nodded fervently as she drew closer. "We would never dare lie to one as powerful as you."

"Hmm... So the mayor did not send these miscreants to try and rob me of my share?"

"Of course not, Lord Grimgrax!" the young woman said, stopping a few feet from the warlock. Her body trembled and her eyes were wide with innocence. "We were prepared to pay everything you asked until the tithe went missing, and we have been scrambling ever since. You must believe that we would never ever think of hiring someone to attack you. We only ask for your mercy while we hunt down the thief."

The warlock frowned. "You have been good subjects over the years. As this is the first misstep that you have made, I shall give you forty-eight hours to find the money. But do not let it happen again! I will not be so kind next time."

"Thank you, Lord Grimgrax!" Adelia bowed low.

The warlock regarded his three would-be-attackers, who were still on the ground, all in various stages of pain. He rolled his eyes at the pathetic sight and vanished from the field.

Adelia let out a loud sigh and visibly relaxed. Looking at the three fallen heroes, she shook her head, disappointed. "I'll let the mayor know what happened."

As the young woman walked away, Aeris couldn't help feeling utterly defeated. She had come here expecting a great victory and was instead handed a terrible defeat. There was no way she could go back to the people of Ironguild with this news, and she doubted that the mayor would give her another chance, not after hearing Adelia's report.

The last of the electricity within her dissipated and she was finally able to stand. "I thought I told you to let me handle this," she said, turning to Corin.

He shrunk at her words. "You... you looked like you needed help," he said, his voice shaking.

"If you two hadn't distracted me, I'd have had him," Grendel growled.

"If you hadn't rushed in-" Corin started, but Grendel glared at him and he instantly stopped speaking, his face managing to go even paler.

"I'm going after him," Grendel declared, hoisting his axe over one shoulder. "And if you two know what's good for you, you'll stay here." He turned and started walking.

"There's no way I'm staying behind," Aeris said, hurrying after him for the second time that day.

Corin said nothing as he followed, holding his book tight against his chest.

Grendel quickly noticed that the two of them were on his tail. He stopped and glared at them. "I'm taking down Grimgrax," he said. "I have the most valid reason—"

"No, *I* do!" Corin interrupted.

Aeris held up her hand. "Hold on, before we start this again we need to deal with something." The others gave her confused looks, but she didn't elaborate. Instead she paused and looked out at the trees which surrounded the clearing. After a few seconds, she strode over to one of the trees and reached out behind it. When her hand reappeared, it was holding onto a small, pale woman with long dark hair, dressed all in black.

"Who are you, and why are you spying on us?" Aeris demanded.

The young woman shrugged sheepishly. "Professional curiosity?"

Grendel's frown deepened and he angrily stalked over.

"Hey!" The woman freed herself of Aeris' grasp and backed up, throwing her hands up in self-defense. "I was sitting in the tavern, minding my own business, when I overheard you two arguing about fighting a warlock. I thought it might be fun to watch – from a distance."

Corin looked genuinely confused as he approached. "That's your idea of fun?"

"Wait a minute!" Grendel trudged over to her and gave her a hard look. "Are you here to fight Grimgrax as well?"

She paused briefly before a determined look crossed her face and she raised a fist in the air. "Yes! My name is Rev... umm... just call me Rev. And I am also here to fight the warlock!"

The other three let out a collective groan. How had one simple task become so complicated?

"Now," Rev continued, "I've noticed that we're all here for the same reason, which has obviously complicated the matter."

"Don't remind me," Grendel muttered.

"Well, since we all want the warlock dead, why don't we work together?" she suggested, smiling brightly.

Aeris looked around at the strange group of humans before her. Corin and Grendel had already proven themselves incapable of working with others, and she doubted that this new person would be much better. If they worked together, it'd be just like what happened earlier. No, she stood a better chance alone.

"I don't work with others," Grendel said angrily. "I don't need any of you messing up my plans."

"I am here on a divine quest," Aeris informed them. "I must insist that you all stay behind while I fight the warlock."

"My quest may not be divine, but it is no less important," Corin said quietly. "I cannot sit by and hope that someone else will succeed."

Rev sighed. "Okay, so nobody wants to work with anyone else. I get it. But we can't all fight Grimgrax alone at the same time. So, how about this? Why don't we all state our case for why we should be the one to perform this deed, and then we hand the task over to the person who most deserves it. Sound good?" She looked at them, a wide smile on her face.

The others looked unconvinced.

"And if that person happens to fail," Rev continued quickly, "we can move on to the next person, and so on, until the warlock's defeated once and for all! How about it?"

Aeris didn't want to waste any more time talking, but she knew that she'd never shake the others without some kind of agreement. They needed to sort this out, and fast.

"I agree," she said.

Corin looked down at the book in his hands and closed his eyes before nodding. "If we must."

Grendel grumbled for a few more seconds before cluing into the fact that he was out-voted. He could sneak away and take on Grimgrax while they wasted time talking, but they might notice that he was missing and come after him. Better to state his reason and get them to agree to back off once and for all.

"Fine," he nodded.

"Excellent," Rev exclaimed. "Let's start with–"

"I'll start, if nobody objects," Aeris interrupted.

"I'll object," Grendel said. "I want to go first."

"Umm..." Corin looked like he really wanted to say something, but there was also fear in his eyes.

Rev sighed again. "We're off to a great start..."

✝

If you'd like to hear Aeris' Tale, continue forward.

Or you can move on to Corin's Tale on Page 25.

Or Grendel's Tale on Page 33.

Or Rev's Tale on Page 37.

Or you can skip all this nonsense
and Journey to Grimgrax's Tower on Page 41.

AERIS' TALE

I've always wanted to help people. Even before I knew what a paladin was, I was living by their code. It's a fortunate thing that I was the fourth-born, because if I'd been first or second-born, my parents never would have let me choose my own path. They'd have expected me to carry on the family business and would never have considered entertaining a different option.

Even as a child, I had a strong sense of right and wrong, and always stuck up for anyone being bullied or taken advantage of. I used to dream about being one of the city guards, and standing as a protector over Eryindale and all its people. It annoyed my siblings to no end, because I never let them get away with anything, but I didn't care. I had a purpose. I was going to protect everyone.

That all changed when I was eleven years old. On that fateful day, I was in the market with my older sister, buying fruit for our parent's bakery. Suddenly a trumpet sounded and a group of people in silver armour marched through the square. They were in two lines, perfectly synchronized, and their spotless armour dazzled in the sunlight. Their heads were held high as they marched, as if they knew that they had been chosen for a higher purpose. Goodness radiated off them, and I became so entranced that I dropped the basket of apples we had just purchased. My sister chased after them as they rolled along the ground, complaining about how I'd ruined all the nice apples she had so carefully picked out. She said father was going to yell at us for bruising them, but I didn't care.

"Who were they?" I said to no one in particular.

"Paladins," the stall owner next to me answered. "From the school in the North of the city. Every once in a while they like to come out and march around the market, looking all pious, but not buying a darn thing. They want to remind us that they're still here, even though we don't have a use for them anymore."

The stall owner didn't sound too impressed with them, but I was entranced. I vowed then and there that I would do whatever it took to become a paladin.

My parents were too busing focusing on my elder siblings' training, so I was allowed to do as I wished. I started my own training schedule, lifting heavy objects and running around the town, and when I turned fourteen I signed up to become a paladin-in-training.

It was both the best and worst thing I'd ever done.

When I entered the school I had been prepared to work hard and prove myself, but I had no idea what was ahead of me. I'd never undergone any formal training before, and although my mind was prepared, my body had never been tested in such ways. Before going to the school, I'd thought I was in good shape, but I was drastically under-prepared for what was to come.

The instructors had us running laps around the school every morning before the sun rose, not allowing us stop until we were ready to fall over with exhaustion. We had to lift heavy objects above our heads and keep them there for as long as possible, receiving disappointed looks and notations in our ledger if we let the objects fall too quickly. My muscles ached with the effort and many times I worried that one day my body would give up and refuse to do the work, and that I would be deemed unworthy and asked to leave.

By this point you're probably wondering why I didn't simply quit and join the city guard instead, and I'd be lying if I told you that very thought didn't cross my mind at least once a day. But those kinds of thoughts are natural to have. You're allowed to have doubts, because doubts are a part of life. If something is difficult then it's okay to wonder if you're actually cut out for it. But you can't let those doubts rule you. If you really want to do something, you shouldn't give up just because it's tough. Most of the time you'd be surprised by how strong you actually are.

Somehow I endured, and after a few months I was pleasantly surprised by how strong I had become. We continued to train hard, and with each day the pain lessened and my strength continued to grow. Even when we sat down to learn about prayers and healing, our muscles cried out, but it was a good ache. One that we knew was for a worthy cause. As time passed, we began training in combat and defensive strategies, and we learned how to best protect others during a fight. We also learned how to avoid a fight, since the best victory is one where you did not have to raise your weapon.

I put in four gruelling years of training and at the end of it all the Grand Master decided that I was strong enough to move on to the Apprentice Level. Elated, I asked what it entailed.

"Go out and do good in the world," he said.

I was confused. "But how?"

He said nothing.

"For how long?"

Still he said nothing.

"But how will I know when I've completed my task? How will I know when I'm ready to move on to the next level?"

I was met only with silence, despite my many questions. A million more inquiries bounced around my head, balancing on the tip of my tongue, ready to spill out. Then, suddenly, I realized what was happening. Being a paladin was not an easy task, so learning how to be one would not be so straightforward. This was not only a task, but also a test.

"Thank you, Grand Master," I said, bowing low. "I will do you and Arete proud."

I received no further instructions before I left, but I knew in my heart what I had to do. I would go out into the world and do good and help people, and when I finally felt that I had earned myself the title of paladin, I would return to the school and prove to my teacher that I was worthy.

However, it would not be so easy. A person can't simply wander around, hoping to stumble upon wrongs that need righting. It can take a lot of time and patience to uncover people in need, and sometimes, by the time you get there, you're too late. But perseverance is key in all things, and so I never lost hope.

My first few quests were small, but still important. I helped negotiate a peace between a wizard and his feline familiar, who was refusing to come down from a tree; I helped stop a tavern from burning down after an overzealous fire in one of their fireplaces got out of hand; and I helped rebuild a family's home after heavy rains caused the roof to collapse. It was enough for me to get a taste of what it was like to help people and spread goodness throughout the world. It was fantastic.

But then I came across the town of Ironguild. They were a small, yet prosperous enough town, mining iron in their nearby caverns and trading all over the province. However, that was before the evil warlock Grimgrax came along and rained his terrible destruction over everything.

Grimgrax seemed to think that they were more prosperous than they actually were and demanded a large tithe in order to 'protect' them. They were a peaceful town and, other than the odd wild animal, they had never needed protection. The mayor tried to explain this to the warlock, innocently saying that they did not require his services. So Grimgrax set fire to the mayor's home to teach them otherwise. He burned down three other houses before explaining that if they could not come up with the tithe in one month, the rest of the town would follow.

The mayor was devastated. Not only did the town not have enough money to pay, but even if they scrimped and saved, it would take at least six months to gather up the amount that Grimgrax was asking for.

It was a mere week after this incident that I stumbled upon this town. After hearing their tale, I felt the call stronger than ever before. This town needed to be protected from the evil cloud hovering over it, and so I swore that I would do my best to help them.

In my search for Grimgrax, I ran across many other towns that had been also been terrorized by the warlock. Indeed, there were not many places within this province that were untouched by his poisonous hand. Although paladins should only raise our swords to protect, I knew that stopping Grimgrax would rid the world of a large amount of evil.

So, when I heard that he would be coming to Quarryville, I immediately headed here. And I would have surely completed my quest if it had not been for your interference, which is why I implore you to leave this to me.

For the sake of the poor, unfortunate people of Ironguild, and all those who suffer under Grimgrax, stand aside and let me finish my quest.

†

Her story finished, Aeris looked at faces that should have been moved to tears by her tale, but were unchanged.

"Well?" she implored, unable to believe that her words had caused no change in their hearts.

Everyone seemed to open their mouths at once.

†

To hear Corin's Tale, continue ahead.

Or move on to Grendel's Tale on Page 33.

Or Rev's Tale on Page 37.

Or you can skip all this nonsense
and Journey to Grimgrax's Tower on Page 41.

CORIN'S TALE

The thing you have to understand is that Wileth was a like a father to me. I already had a family, but by the time I met Wileth, they weren't paying me much notice. My mother and father wanted me to be a great fighter, like they had been and like my two older brothers were, but I didn't care for fighting. What I truly loved was reading.

My entire family was embarrassed by my pacifist hobby and when I was younger they did everything they could to try and discourage me. If they found a book in the house they would toss it on the fire or tear it to shreds, and if they caught me reading they would punish me with physical labour.

Despite this, I never stopped reading and never lost my love of books. As time passed, my parents eventually gave up trying to force me into physical training

– partly because of how stubborn I was, and partly because it became apparent that I'd never be a good fighter, let alone a great one. I tried my best, but fighting didn't come easy to me, and I always seemed to be tripping up over my own feet. After many classes and demonstrations, my parents realized that it would be more embarrassing to continue to force me to fight than it would be to let me give up and read.

The arraignment was made, and while they allowed me to remain under their roof, they essentially disowned me, excluding me from family outings and leaving me to eat my meals alone. But that was okay because I was finally allowed to choose my own path.

I kept to myself and tried my best to stay out of everyone's way. Eventually I'd have to think about how to make a living through my love of reading, but for now all I wanted was to absorb as much information from as many books as possible.

When Wileth first saw me, it was in the library in my town. It was a small building, barely bigger than a living room, and not many people used it. Most of the books were magical in nature, so many of the visitors were wizards and sorcerers. I had no magical abilities, but I was eager to read anything I could get my hands on. It was also a good place to hide from the rest of the town. I would frequently go inside, grab a book, and sit and read all day. And that is how Wileth found me.

"Training to be a wizard, are you?" he asked.

His voice startled me and I dropped the book, losing my place. Looking up at the imposing stranger, somehow I managed to squeak out an answer. "Not particularly..."

"Then why are you reading about magical attacks?"

"Um..." I looked at the book. "It was here?"

A look of exasperation crossed his face. "Do you have any interest in spells or casting?"

"Um... Well... I hadn't really given it much thought." The only reason I'd picked up the book was because I hadn't read it yet – the contents were entirely incidental.

"Tell me," Wileth said, his voice curt, "have you retained anything from this book which you seem to be so engrossed in?"

I'm sure a look of pure terror crossed my face. He grabbed the book and flipped through it.

"What is the purpose of Enver's Frost?" he asked.

I froze, terrified by being put on the spot. He sighed and started to walk away, but I somehow managed to find my voice before he got too far.

"Enver's Frost is a ranged attack that holds and freezes multiple enemies," I said.

He stopped in his tracks and turned around, a smile crossing his face. "Well then. Perhaps there's more to you than a pair of eyes."

We talked for almost an hour. His full name was Wileth Onyxside and he was a wizard. He lived in a nearby village, and had come here to see what kind of books we had in our library. 'Sometimes the best discoveries can be found in the strangest places' he would often tell me. When he noticed that I was reading that particular book, he'd had a thought that maybe I was looking for someone to teach me how to be a wizard, and then he thought that maybe it was time for him to get an apprentice.

When I think back to how I'd almost ruined that

moment, how close I came to not being who I am now, well, it's almost enough to make me lose sleep.

Wileth told me what it was like to study wizardry and how you didn't need any innate magic to train, and I suddenly realized that I could put my love of reading to practical use. I also realized that this was my chance to get away from my family once and for all. They'd be happier with me gone, and surely I'd be much happier living with Wileth. Despite not having known him for very long, he seemed nice enough. It probably wouldn't be a good idea to cross him, but at least he wouldn't pretend I didn't exist.

Deciding to go with Wileth changed my life. I finally learned what it was like for someone to care about my hopes and dreams, and to encourage me in something I cared about. If I failed at a task, Wileth would of course be disappointed, but it was never as bad as my parents and their disappointment in my not being a fighter. And I could always make him happy by eventually succeeding.

Wileth became my true family. I looked up to him as if he had been my father and I know that he regarded me fondly. We were truly happy.

It all went terribly wrong a few years later. Wileth had sent me to a nearby village on a supply run, gathering some exotic spell ingredients that we'd run out of. It was a journey that I had made many times before, but this trip was to be different.

Everything seemed fine until my return. I was drawing close to home when I suddenly noticed smoke. At first I thought that Wileth had made a fire in anticipation of my return, to boil up a new potion, but then I noticed that the grey cloud was growing larger and darker, and I knew that this was not a normal fire.

I raced home to discover that our storage shed was in flames. Wileth wasn't in sight, but it looked as if there had been a battle, with broken branches and smoldering trees. The door to our home was shattered. Quickly, I raced into the house, calling out his name. Inside I could tell that there had been a fight – a bad one. Most of the furniture in the common room had been broken, shattered bottles were all over the floor, and our belongings were scattered everywhere instead of being neatly stored on the shelves.

My heart starting beating faster as I looked around frantically, calling for Wileth. Finally I heard a noise from the study. Inside, I saw Wileth lying amongst the wreckage of his desk, blood pooling beneath him. I knelt down next to him and accessed the damage. He was still alive, but just barely. His breathing was shallow and the pool of blood continued to grow.

"I'll get a healing potion," I told him, but as I turned away I felt a hand grab my arm, holding me back. When I turned I saw that it was Wileth. I have no idea how he had that much strength still left in him.

"Grimgrax..." he rasped. "Don't–"

His hand fell from my arm and I knew he was gone.

Later, after burying Wileth behind the house and saying my goodbyes, I set about my new purpose. When I asked around the village, I learned who Grimgrax was and what he did, and I knew that I had to stop him. So I gathered up my supplies and set off, vowing revenge for what he'd done.

†

Corin felt emotionally drained at the end of his story. Not much time had passed since it had happened and every moment was still fresh in his memory.

"Don't?"

He turned to Grendel. "What?"

"Your teacher's last word was 'don't'," Grendel said flatly.

Corin nodded. "That's what it sounded like."

"Has it occurred to you that he might have been telling you not to go after Grimgrax? As in 'Don't seek him out'?"

Corin was taken aback. "No, not really. I mean, why would he have said such a thing?"

"Maybe because he was a much stronger wizard than you and Grimgrax defeated him, so what chance could you possibly have?" Grendel crossed his arms over his chest, his point made.

"He might have been telling me, 'Don't let him get away with this.' Did you think of that?"

"I'm inclined to agree with Grendel," Aeris spoke up. "I think it's more logical that he was trying to protect you and wanted to stop you from going on a potentially fatal mission."

"But you don't know that for sure," Corin counter-ed.

"And you don't know that he didn't!" Grendel shot back.

Corin could feel anger building up inside of him. His face felt hot and he knew that his voice was rising higher and higher with every word. Closing his eyes, he took a few deep breaths and calmed himself down.

"Tell me, all of you," he began, his voice much

calmer than before. "If your mentor – the one person who was like family to you, the one person you could trust – died, would you sit at home and not seek vengeance? Even if they told you not to? This is why I should be the one to go after Grimgrax."

He'd thought that his story would move the others enough that they would step aside, but they looked just as determined as before.

†

To hear Grendel's Tale, continue forward.

Or you can move on to Rev's Tale on Page 37.

Or you go back to Aeris' Tale on Page 17.

Or you can skip all this nonsense
and Journey to Grimgrax's Tower on Page 41.

GRENDEL'S TALE

I don't care about your stories. They could all be exactly the same as mine and I still wouldn't care.

The thing you need to realize is that I never intended on becoming a fighter. I was perfectly content in my previous life, spending my days farming and tending to the family fields. If it hadn't been for that horrible warlock, I'd still be there. And I'd be happy. I would have married one of the local girls, probably Zozanna, and would have raised children who would grow up and work the fields with me. And we'd drink tea in the evenings and look up at the stars, and eat bread made from the wheat we'd grown. It would have been enough.

But that was before Grimgrax targeted my village. We weren't rich, but we had some savings, in case anything happened to the village. We managed to purchase safety a couple of years in a row, but it cost us almost everything. Our savings dwindled, and despite having good harvests, there came a year that we weren't able to raise enough. Our mayor tried to pay the remainder with goods like food and pottery, but Grimgrax scorned the effort and said that if we had the ability to make things, then we should be making money.

The warlock said that he would give the mayor two days to come up with the money or he would show us exactly what he was protecting us from.

Well, threats can't make money magically appear from nowhere, so we were at a loss. The mayor told us not to worry and said that we should go back to our homes and relax. She would handle everything. I felt strange watching her say this, because although she was trying to seem strong and determined, there was something not right about her demeanour. Later I realized that she was resigned and scared. I think her plan was to offer her life in exchange for our safety.

When Grimgrax came back, I was busy working in the fields. It was mid-afternoon and I had been cutting wheat since the morning. It was peaceful out there, and all of my worries quickly disappeared with each swing of the scythe. All that existed for me was the sound of wheat being shorn, the feel of the scythe's wooden handle in my hands, and the birds twittering. I'd never realized that it was nearing the time of the warlock's return, despite the location of the sun in the sky.

Then the birds went quiet. Shortly after that, a scream pierced the air. When I looked up, I noticed smoke rising from the direction of my village. More screams sounded as fires erupted everywhere. I dropped the scythe and ran towards my house, but before I could reach it, it exploded in flames. I was thrown backwards and everything went black.

When I woke up it was too late. The village had been burned to the ground and almost everyone was dead, including my family.

†

He looked at each of them. "Until you've felt a loss as big as mine, do not presume to tell me how I should pity you. I have worked hard and trained hard so that when I finally go up against Grimgrax I will kill him or die trying. And none of you will stop me in my quest."

When he finished speaking, the others remained silent. He knew that his story had touched them and that they would be fools to tell him to stay behind.

"Just because Wileth was not my blood-father, it does not mean that his death affected me any less," Corin said quietly.

"And Grimgrax has done the same to many others," Aeris added. "You are not alone in your feelings, Grendel." He glared at her, but she did not stop talking. "You say that you are willing to die in your attempt to defeat Grimgrax, but that is exactly why we cannot let you be the one to go against him. If you die, Grimgrax will continue his reign of terror. We need someone who will stop this man, no matter what."

Grendel growled. "How dare you say such a thing to me?"

"I am not thinking of you, but of every village in

this province."

He growled again, but did not respond.

Rev laughed nervously. "So, who's up next?"

†

To hear what Rev's Tale is, continue forward.

If you'd like, you can go back to
Aeris' Tale on Page 17.

Or go back to Corin's Tale on Page 25.

Or you can skip all this nonsense
and Journey to Grimgrax's Tower on Page 41.

REV'S TALE

As all eyes turned to her, Rev considered what she was going to say.

Should she tell them the truth? That she wasn't here to kill Grimgrax, but instead to steal his staff once one of the others had dispatched him? That if the paladin hadn't discovered her, she'd still be hiding in the trees, watching them, and would have followed them all the way to the warlock's tower to loot the riches that lay within?

Should she try to gain their trust by telling them of her difficult childhood? How she'd grown up in a wealthy family that expected her to be a perfect little lady – seen but not heard. How her parents expected her to be obedient at all times, and not have a single original thought in her head. Maybe she could tell them how alive she'd felt when she began stealing, and how for the first time in her life she could feel the blood pumping through her veins as she was filled with an emotion other than boredom.

Or maybe she could try to gain their pity by talking about how her parents had turned her away once they learned of her less-than-desirable hobby, taking away the only home she'd ever known and cutting her off from her siblings. It had been difficult for her, to have come from so much and suddenly to have to so little, and there had been many hungry days and cold nights. She'd had to learn a lot of hard lessons to survive, but survive she did.

Or maybe she could lie – tell them about a made-up family that had been murdered or a town that had been destroyed – something that would put her on equal footing with the rest of them. But she didn't actually want them to let her fight Grimgrax alone. They were the fighters, not her. She wanted to tag along, to be there when the warlock fell, and to gather up all those wonderful treasures that would no doubt fetch a good price at market.

Maybe she could pretend to be a bard and express her wishes to follow along, eager to compose countless songs about the downfall of the miserable warlock Grimgrax. Too bad she had no instrument and couldn't carry a tune.

Taking in a deep breath, she thought about the pros and cons of all her options and made her choice.

†

"Honestly," she finally said, "my story will not convince you of anything. You have all made up your minds and no amount of words will change them. We all know that Grimgrax is terrible and needs to be stopped, and no amount of talking will lessen any of our reasons for hating him. So why don't we make a decision already and get on with it?"

†

To Journey to Grimgrax's Tower, continue forward.

Or you can go back to Aeris' Tale on Page 17.

Or back to Corin's Tale on Page 25.

Or back to Grendel's Tale on Page 33.

THE JOURNEY TO GRIMGRAX'S TOWER

"Talking this over is a stupid idea and a complete waste of time," Grendel scowled.

Aeris couldn't help agreeing, although she didn't like the way he'd phrased it. "It's obvious that we are all too resolved to give up on our quests. The longer we stand here and discuss the matter, the more time Grimgrax has to harm others."

"Well, we're at an impasse then," Rev replied. "So let's look at our options, shall we? We can either go after Grimgrax alone, but with everyone else around us, and have a repeat of that hilarious performance from a few minutes ago. Or, we can reconsider working together."

Corin, Grendel, and Aeris frowned.

Rev gave them an encouraging smile. "Just think about it. I know that you all got in each other's way back there, but if you actually worked together and fought as a team, surely you'd be able to defeat Grimgrax. He'd have a much harder time going up against the three of you, after all."

"Don't you mean the four of us?" Corin said, confused.

Rev laughed. "Of course that's what I meant. If we work together, the *four* of us can take down Grimgrax and achieve all of our dreams. No matter what happens, if we all have a hand in the fight, then we'll all have had a part in defeating him. The power of teamwork, etcetera, etcetera..." She widened her smile, hoping that her positive attitude would be enough to win them over. Sure enough, it seemed like a couple of them were actually considering it.

"She may have a point," Aeris said slowly, the words uncomfortable in her mouth.

"You can't be serious!" Grendel blurted out, throwing his hands in the air.

Corin shrugged. "It's a matter of numbers, really, if you think about it. Four against one should yield a better chance of success than one against one."

Grendel growled and narrowed his eyes.

Aeris moved as if to put a hand on his shoulder, but wisely stopped and let her hand fall to her side. "I know you're determined to follow your own path, Grendel, but if you really want to honour your family's memory, you'll put an end to the warlock's terror no matter what it takes. Deep down, you don't want anyone else to ever feel pain like you've felt, which means that you'll do the right thing and stop Grimgrax, even if it means working with us to do it."

His frown deepened, and for a moment she wondered if he'd turn on all of them, preferring their deaths over their help. Not only did she not want to fight him, but a battle would waste a lot of time and energy. She wondered if there was something she could say to convince him to join their side, but then he gave a huff and his posture relaxed.

"Fine," he said. "But we need to get going. Now."

"Then let's move on!" Rev exclaimed, gesturing for the others to start walking. Grendel took the lead, with Aeris only a few steps behind. Corin stayed behind Aeris, holding his book tightly, and Rev took up the rear. They walked for a few steps before Rev cleared her throat. "We all know how to find Grimgrax's tower, right?" she said.

"Of course," Grendel replied impatiently. "His tower is in the South."

"Just checking!"

They were silent as they walked. The only sounds were that of leaves rustling in the wind, far-off animals in the surrounding woods, and their footsteps along the well-worn path. Occasionally they would hear Grendel muttering under his breath or Corin whispering the properties of various spells, but there was no actual conversation.

Although she was relieved that they'd come to an arrangement, Aeris knew that it wasn't enough that they'd agreed to work together – they needed to come up with an actual plan. Grimgrax was strong and deceptive, and if they didn't agree on how to fight him, he'd certainly win again.

"We should make a list of our strengths and

weaknesses," Aeris said out loud. "Then we'll know what jobs we're each best suited for and we can come up with a proper plan of attack."

"Well," Corin started hesitantly, "I'm good at spells and casting, but not actual hand-to-hand combat."

"I'm not as good a fighter as some of you, but I'm creative and a quick thinker," Rev said.

Grendel sighed loudly. "I'm good at knowing that Grimgrax needs to suffer, and my weakness is that I have all of you holding me back."

Aeris chose to ignore his hostility. "It would make sense for Grendel and me to go on the offense. That way Corin can stay back and cast spells, and Rev can..." She paused. "Rev, what exactly is it that you can do?"

"Umm..." Rev paused. "I guess you could call me a creative thinker. Problem solver, even."

"But what does that mean?"

"Well, I'm pretty helpful with locked doors and making sure that rooms are safe, and finding items that might come in handy..." she trailed off.

Corin held back a laugh. "You're a rogue."

Rev shrugged and tried to look innocent.

"A rogue?" Aeris was astonished, but once she started to think about it, it made sense. After all, she'd discovered Rev hiding in the forest, spying on them. And her dark outfit was well suited to someone who spent their time sneaking around in shadows.

Never in her entire life, did Aeris ever expect herself to be working with a common thief. How could she risk tarnishing her reputation by working alongside someone with such low morals? What if the Grand Master found out? Would it disqualify her from becoming a true paladin?

She almost stopped dead in her tracks, but then her gaze fell on Grendel. He was also rough around the edges and not her first choice for a partner, but he had a valid reason for wanting to fight Grimgrax. Although there might not be much nobility in a person, there could be nobility in their actions, and although she knew nothing of Rev's motivations, if she wanted to defeat Grimgrax then it should be enough.

"Well..." Aeris said, trying to maintain her composure, "I'm sure that there's something we can find for you to do during the fight..." She tried to think of the skills a Rogue would have, but stealing Grimgrax's belongings probably wouldn't help them.

"Oh!" Corin's eyes lit up. "Maybe she could steal Grimgrax's staff. I be he'd be less powerful without it."

Grendel scoffed. "Yeah, like that's going to be easy to do."

Aeris sighed. "Grendel, I know that you're unhappy with this situation, but could you please try to be helpful? I know that this is not how any of us wanted to go about our task, but we should be thankful that we have allies, not resentful."

Grendel laughed bitterly.

"You know what? That's enough!" Aeris stopped walking and stamped her foot down on the path. "Grendel, if you do not wish to work with us, then I will be forced to make you stay behind. I cannot risk your pride getting in the way."

He turned on her. "How dare you threaten me?"

"I have vowed to help the people of this province and I will not let anybody stand in my way. Not even you."

Crossing his arms, he sneered at her. "And how do you expect to make me stay behind?"

Rev cleared her throat. "I have some rope in my pack. We could tie him to a tree."

Aeris held back a smile. "Now, Grendel, this is your final chance. Do you wish to work with us or against us?"

Although she was uncertain if the three of them would be able to contain the fighter, she could see that the threat was doing its job. Grendel's face registered a multitude of expressions as he quickly contemplated the best course of action.

Corin watched hesitantly, unsure whether he wanted ed Grendel to go with them or have him stay behind, while Rev stood off to the side, trying to remember how much rope she had in her possession.

"Grendel?" Aeris prompted carefully. "What is your answer?"

He scowled and his arms fell to his side. "I want Grimgrax to pay for his crimes. I want to see his face at the moment he realizes that he's been defeated. And if that means I have to pretend to be happy about working with you, then I will do it." He sighed and seemed to deflate a little. "Let's get back on the path. We can go over the plan while we walk."

As they started walking again, Aeris found it difficult to contain her smile. For the first time since this mission began, she finally felt a glimmer of hope.

THE TOWER OF EVIL

The four of them looked up at the imposing structure before them. It looked like an evil tower should, with blackened stones, crumbling mortar, thin windows, and dark ivy creeping upwards. It rose into the clouds like a monolith, making it impossible to tell how tall it was.

They were standing well away from it, at the entrance of the small clearing where the tower had been built. The path they'd taken to get there was over-grown, possibly due to Grimgrax's ability to teleport in and out, and it had taken them longer than expected to reach their destination. Luckily, if they ever doubted that they were heading the right way, all they needed to do was look up and see the dark structure towering in the distance.

Although they'd finally agreed on a plan for fighting the warlock, they hadn't thought about what they'd do once they reached the tower, nor about the obstacles that they might find in their way. The path to the door seemed clear, but now that the terrible tower was in front of them, it didn't feel wise to simply walk up to it.

"This seems too easy," Aeris said softly. She doubted that the warlock was hiding in the woods, spying on them, but it was better to be safe than sorry.

"There are probably traps," Grendel said.

"It'd make sense," Rev nodded. "Ol' Grimmy doesn't seem like the type to welcome uninvited company."

"So, what do we do now?" Corin asked as he stared up at the tower, his face a mix of determination and concern.

Rev narrowed her eyes and looked around. "Give me a second to see if I can find anything suspicious."

Grendel rolled his eyes, picked up a small rock, and threw it at the ground near the tower's door. It landed and bounced a few times. Nothing happened.

"Don't trust me?" Rev remarked.

"Don't trust anyone but myself," Grendel replied.

"Well, if you set off a trap while I'm near it, I'll give you a darn good reason not to trust me."

The two of them glared at each other and Aeris found herself stepping in between them.

"Let's give Rev a chance to look for traps," she said diplomatically. "And if Grendel's not satisfied with her results, he can toss as many stones as he'd like once she's done."

Grendel sighed but didn't argue, which Aeris took as a win. She gestured for Rev to start hunting for traps.

While the rogue slowly made her way towards the tower's door, Aeris looked up at the structure again. The reality of where they were finally hit her and she felt her heart start to beat faster. She wanted to march up to the tower, find Grimgrax, and end his reign of terror once and for all, but it might not be that simple. It was possible that they'd fall into a trap or that Grimgrax would be ready and waiting for them or that he might not even be home. If only they'd been able to work together better in Quarryville, then maybe they'd have defeated him there. Hopefully they could defeat him now.

A low whistle interrupted her thoughts and she looked in the direction of the noise. Rev was standing next to the tower's door, waving them over. Aeris looked over at Grendel, who picked up a handful of rocks and tossed them towards the door, rolling them along the ground. Nothing happened, other than Rev shooting him a dirty look as a few came barrelling her way. Despite this, Grendel still didn't look satisfied. A quick glance at Corin showed that he was also still concerned, so Aeris squared her shoulders and walked a straight line towards Rev.

Each step made her heart beat faster. She expected something to jump out at her or come barrelling towards her, but nothing happened. The entire walk to the tower was unremarkable. A sense of dread filled her stomach. How could it be this easy?

Grendel and Corin quickly joined her, walking the exact same path. As they stood before the door, all eyes were on her, and Aeris realized that she'd become the de facto leader. Hopefully they'd be willing to follow her this loyally once the fighting started.

She reached out for the doorknob and tried to turn it, but it wouldn't move. She tried again, but the doorknob still refused to budge.

"Leave it to me," Rev smiled, cracking her knuckles. She pulled some tools out of one of her belt pouches and in less than a minute the door was unlocked. It gave a slight creak as she pushed it open.

All four of them peered inside. Aeris didn't know what she expected, but this seemed appropriate. A round, empty room, illuminated by blue light coming from magical torches on the wall. The floor was covered with a thin layer of dirt and dust, and although there were faint footprints and tracks, it was difficult to know if they had been made weeks, months, or even years ago.

"No traps that I can see," Rev whispered.

Aeris slowly stepped forward, bracing herself for an attack, but one never came. Standing in the middle of the room, she noticed a stone staircase that started on her left and wound up around the wall, disappearing into the upper level. There were no sounds coming from above. If Grimgrax was home, how far up the tower might he be? How far would they have to climb? And would there be any traps awaiting them?

"So..." Rev said quietly. "Going up?"

"I guess so," Aeris replied.

"And what do we do if Grimmy isn't home?"

She paused to think. "We could lie in wait," she said uncertainly. "Maybe set a trap. We'll figure something out."

She didn't want to say it, but the ease of their approach was causing her to wonder if they had the right place. It was possible that Grimgrax had lied about his tower's location in order to fool any would-be attackers. Sure there were glowing torches and the front door had been locked, but what if it was all a ruse? What if some other magic-user lived here?

What if they climbed all the way to the top of the tower and there was no sign of Grimgrax anywhere? Should they stay here in the vain hope that they had the right tower or would it be smarter to move on and try to find the warlock somewhere else? Although she had been more than ready to take on Grimgrax, never had she imagined that she would end up being responsible for the well-being of three other people. Nobody else wanted to step up as the leader and she was worried that without someone taking point in this strange group, they'd all go back to doing their own thing and get in each other's ways again. She'd taken up the mantle because someone had to, and sometimes being the leader meant acting confident even if you weren't certain what the heck you were doing.

Taking in a deep breath, Aeris pushed aside her doubts and motioned for the others to follow her up the staircase. Even if they found nothing here, they still had to try. She would search every single part of this tower and confirm that the warlock was nowhere in sight before giving up.

They walked up the staircase as quietly as possible, but it was difficult to stop the occasional scuff of boots on stone or the metallic clang of armour and weapons. Aeris kept an eye out for any doors in the stone wall, but there were no openings anywhere, other than the occasional window. After what felt like too long of a climb, she finally spied an opening. Motioning for everyone to stop, she moved forward on her own. Cautiously, she peered into the room, but it was completely empty. Taking a closer look, she saw that there was nothing but undisturbed dust on the floor and cobwebs hanging along the walls. Aeris tried to reassure herself that it wouldn't be smart for someone with so many enemies to use the first room in such a tall tower, but she could feel her doubts growing.

Still, she pushed onward. The second opening wasn't as far away as the first had been. Looking inside, she saw that the room wasn't entirely empty, but that the chairs and table scattered around were just as dust-covered as the previous room.

"Umm..." Corin said hesitantly. "Are we sure—"

She quickly shushed him before he could finish that thought. She needed to believe that this was Grimgrax's tower and that he was somewhere inside. Despite her own very real doubts, she knew that if they turned back now, she'd always wonder if the next room had been the right one, or the one after that.

Corin fell silent and they continued upward. Aeris almost didn't want to look at the next room, fearful that it would be more dust and disappointment, but when she peeked inside she felt hope rising within. There was nobody in the room, but it was filled with herbs. There were shelves covered in jars of dried herbs, tables holding pots of fresh herbs, and leafy green bundles hanging from the ceiling. The sight of the fresh potted plants meant that someone had to come here often enough to tend for them. Even if it wasn't Grimgrax, somebody definitely lived here.

With a renewed confidence, Aeris pressed on. The next room was filled with books – thick, leather bound novels, with no titles written on the spines or covers. She could see Corin staring at the books, longing for enough time to sit and read them all, but she kept the group moving. Maybe, once all this was over, she would let him take some of the books. After all, once they had completed their plan, Grimgrax would no longer need them. The following room had shelves filled with jars of assorted items, some suspended in liquid, some ground into powder, none of them labelled. The room seemed to radiate a dark power and she quickly pressed on.

The energy of the building became more oppressive as they climbed. It felt like they were getting closer, like Grimgrax was up there somewhere, waiting for them. Aeris indicated to the group that they should be extra quiet as they continued. She had no idea how high the staircase went, but hopefully they wouldn't have to go much further. Her legs were already beginning to tire.

The next room was filled with tables, each with assorted items laid out. The items looked as if they had been carefully placed, perhaps in preparation for spell creation. A small part of her wanted to mess with everything in the room, so that she would mess up whatever the warlock was working on, but there were more important things waiting ahead. Also, it was always a bad idea for a person to mess with magic they knew nothing about.

As they approached the next doorway, Aeris heard a sound like liquid bubbling. She told the others to wait and carefully moved forward. Looking in, she confirmed that someone was inside the room, standing in front of a large, boiling cauldron. The person's back was to her and they didn't seem to have noticed her approach. Despite the fact that she couldn't see the person's face, she could tell by the dark red robes and long dark hair that it had to be Grimgrax.

Aeris moved away from the door and quietly pulled out her sword before motioning for the others to ready their weapons. She gave a determined nod to the group and they all nodded back at her. Grendel finally stopped scowling and took in a deep steadying breath. Corin looked nervous and shaken, but his eyes held strength. Rev actually started to smile. Aeris said a quick prayer to her god and hoped that everyone would stick to the plan.

The group clustered around the door and quietly started to file into the room. Aeris and Corin went off to the left, while Grendel and Rev moved to the right. They crept closer.

"I really should put more security on that door," a familiar, booming voice declared.

The group froze. The figure in front of the cauldron hadn't moved, but there was no doubt that it was Grimgrax who had spoken.

"Then again," the figure slowly turned around, revealing his wicked smile, "if I did that, I wouldn't get to punish those who mistakenly wandered in."

Their plan immediately fell apart.

Grendel lunged for the warlock while Rev ducked underneath a nearby desk. As Corin flinched and stepped backwards, Aeris abandoned his side and leaped forward, trying to catch up to Grendel's momentum. Grimgrax aimed a bolt of electricity towards Grendel, knocking him back into the wall, before turning on her. She was too far away to strike him, but she managed to block his attack with her shield. Taking the quickest glance possible behind her, she could see a shimmering blue around Corin's hands as he opened up a scroll. She needed to keep the warlock's attention away from him for as long as possible.

She moved to the right and stepped forward. Grimgrax's next attack pushed her back, but she maintained a strong hold on her shield and didn't let it knock her down. Grimgrax let out a growl and she could see fire in his red eyes as he prepared another spell. She prayed for the strength of Arete to fill her, but before she could finish the prayer, Grimgrax sent a pillar of fire her way.

Her shield blocked the blast, directing the fire away from her, but the attack was unending. Sweat formed on her forehead as the air around her grew hot and the fire heated up her shield. The temperature was almost too much to bear and she felt her legs start to weaken as even her armour began to heat up. She had to do something, but if she tried to move forward, surely the heat would get worse, and if she moved backwards, she'd soon come up against the wall. How much longer could this spell possibly last?

The fire suddenly stopped and Aeris fell to her knees, the cool air bringing a welcome relief. She looked up and saw that Grimgrax was frantically look- ing around, one hand rubbing the back of his head.

"Who did that!?" he snarled. "Where are you?"

Corin was still working on the scroll, and although she was tired, Aeris knew she had to get back into the fight before Grimgrax noticed what he was up to. Bracing her sword against the floor, she used it to help herself stand up. Although her body ached from that last attack, she knew that there wasn't enough time to rest.

A loud roar caught her attention and she saw Grendel rush forward with his axe raised. By the time Grimgrax turned toward the sound, Grendel was too close for him to do anything but bring his staff up to block the swinging axe.

Aeris felt a tremendous sense of relief at the sight of Grendel. His attack was exactly what she needed to give her time to regain some of her strength before jumping back into the fight. She looked around for Rev but couldn't see her anywhere. Perhaps the rogue had hidden somewhere in the room, or maybe it had become too much for her and she'd fled. No matter what had become of her, Aeris knew that she had to push on.

Grendel was doing a good job holding his own against Grimgrax, but eventually the warlock found an opportunity. Pushing the axe to the side, he knocked Grendel back with another jolt of electricity, sending him to the floor. However, Aeris had been waiting for this moment. She saw the warlock's eyes finally notice Corin across the room, but then she was yelling, coming for him with her sword raised and he had to block it with his staff.

This time she was prepared for the resistance that the staff offered and, gritting her teeth, she held her ground. Their weapons locked together, the two of them straining under the effort. She was thinking of her next move when a book flew towards Grimgrax, hitting him in the head. Aeris used the opportunity to crouch down and sweep Grimgrax's legs out from under him, sending him to the floor. His staff fell from his hands as he tried to catch himself, landing hard on the stone floor. By the time he looked up, both Aeris and Grendel had their weapons trained on him.

"Wait!" Grimgrax said. "You've bested me in combat, which is no small feat. If you leave now, I promise not to take revenge on any of you."

"I don't think you're in any position to make such a bargain," Grendel said, his eyes cold and narrow.

"We're not here to best you," Aeris added. "We're here to stop you from harming innocent people and taking all their money."

"And what if I promise to stop?" Grimgrax said.

Aeris always tried to see the good in people, but she didn't trust him one bit. "I doubt that you're capable of keeping such a promise."

"Besides, you still need to pay for your past crimes," Grendel replied harshly.

"What about the crimes that were done to me?" Grimgrax fired back. "My past was not an easy one, yet those people never paid for what they did to me."

"We don't care."

Grimgrax looked at Aeris. "I'll bet that your paladin cares about right and wrong, and would never leap into action without hearing someone's side of the story."

He smiled kindly at her and Aeris felt her stomach turn. He was right. Being a paladin meant always doing the right thing, and although she doubted that he would say anything that would absolve him of his crimes, could she act without proper knowledge?

"So," Grimgrax asked, "what do you say?"

†

To hear Grimgrax's Tragic Past, continue forward.

Or if you don't care about Grimgrax's past,
jump to The Battle's End on Page 63.

GRIMGRAX'S TRAGIC PAST

"Fine," Aeris sighed. "Let us hear your tale before passing judgment." She hoped she wouldn't regret this.

Beside her, Grendel huffed, but he said nothing and continued holding his axe steady on the warlock.

Despite the weapons pointed at him, Grimgrax relaxed.

"All my life I have had to fight adversity. To say that my childhood was difficult would be an understatement. I never knew who my father was, and to this day I still do not know. On this matter, the people of my town have had plenty of speculation about who he might have been, but their ideas always involved scandal or shame. My mother refused to tell anyone who my father was, including me. No matter how many times I begged or pleaded, she kept that information secret.

"In a village of happy families and familial pride, this made me an outcast. Nobody said anything to my face, but I heard the whispers and rumours, and saw how they all looked at me. I lived in a perpetual state of never fitting in, and the townsfolk were more than happy to keep it that way.

"It got worse as I grew older, as I discovered my true power. I could always feel the magic inside of me, but when I was a child I had no idea what it was. Strange things would happen when I was around, but I had no idea if I was causing it nor how to control it. People began to say that I was cursed, that my father had been some kind of demon and I would bring destruction and bad luck to the town. My mother denied this and told me that I could be a force of good for the world if I wanted to, but still she remained quiet about who my father had been, leaving me with only questions and shame.

"Finally, when I was ten years old I found a book about magic in the library and realized that all of my bad luck was due to untamed magical potential. So I studied hard and learned how to control my power. But the townspeople didn't care about the truth, nor did they want to acknowledge that the strange things had stopped happening. No matter how much I tried to convince them that my 'curse' was under control, they still blamed every random bad happenstance on me. If an animal died, it was my fault. Every bad storm, every accident, every time a person tripped up... My mother told me that they were jealous of my power and that I should use my power to show them how good I could be, but she had no idea what it was like to be me and to have to endure their horrible gossip.

"After a few more years of this, I made a decision. I was going to show these people just how bad their luck could get. I would make them regret every terrible thing they'd ever said about me or my father. If they dared to think that a thunderstorm had been caused by me, then I would conjure up the worst thunderstorm they'd ever seen!"

It was as if he'd forgotten that they were there. The longer he talked, the more his face fell into a deep scowl and the brighter his eyes burned with hatred. When he talked about thunder, Aeris heard pure delight in his voice, and she couldn't help wondering what terrible things he had done to those villagers.

"Umm…" Rev said, her hesitant voice coming out from the shadows, "was that supposed to make us want to leave you alone? Because that was super evil."

THE BATTLE'S END

"It doesn't matter," Corin spoke up. "The spell's done."

"What spell?" Grimgrax asked, his voice flat and threatening.

A large smile broke out on Corin's face. "The binding spell that I cast on you. You've been cut off from your magic."

Disbelief crossed the warlock's face, but it was soon replaced with anger. His right hand, which had been creeping across the floor, reached out for his staff, but it was no longer there. His eyes widened as Rev walked out from the shadows, the staff in her left hand.

"Looking for this?" she smirked.

"But..."

"It doesn't matter," Corin informed him, taking a

few steps closer. "Even the magic in your staff won't respond to you. You will never harm anyone through magic ever again."

Grimgrax's eyes burned, but there was no actual fire to accompany his glare, no matter how hard he tried to conjure it. "You may think you have me beat, but you are wrong. I will spend the rest of my life breaking these bonds, and when I do I will hunt down each and every one of you and destroy you."

"And that is why I have this second scroll," Corin smiled, drawing another scroll from his satchel.

Grimgrax moved forward, but Grendel's axe quickly blocked him, the sharp edge uncomfortably close to the warlock's throat.

"Just give me one reason…" Grendel said quietly, his eyes narrowing.

Corin made quick work of the second scroll and the spell was soon cast. As soon as Corin stopped talking, Grimgrax's body relaxed and calm fell over him. His eyes glazed over and his expression went neutral.

"That should do it," Corin said, tucking the used scrolls away.

Aeris lowered her sword and indicated to Grendel that he should do the same. She knelt down next to the dazed former warlock.

"How are you?" she asked Grimgrax carefully.

His eyes, which had turned grey, came into focus and he looked around the room uncertainly. "I… I think I am fine. Who are you? Where are we?" His voice sounded higher and lighter.

"You wandered into someone's tower by accident, and it looks like you've had a terrible fall. Would you like us to show you the way out?"

"Oh. Oh, yes. I think that would be best."

Aeris held out her hand and helped Grimgrax to his feet. It felt strange to be offering any kind of help to someone who had been so wicked, but the change in his demeanour was so drastic that it was difficult to find him even the slightest bit terrifying anymore. Before leaving the tower, she'd convinced him to cut his hair and change out of the dark red robe, and now that he was wearing a simple tunic and trousers, he looked more like a shopkeeper than a blood-thirsty warlock. Grimgrax was gone, replaced by an odd, confused man.

Once they were out of the tower, she pointed him in the direction of the nearest town, gave him a few coins, and sent him on his way.

"Are we sure this is better?" Grendel asked as they watched Grimgrax wander away, his confused gaze taking in all of his surroundings. "What if he remembers who he is? What if he breaks the binding spell?"

"If he manages to do that," Aeris replied, "then we will hunt him down and bind him again."

The new and improved Grimgrax finally disappeared from view, yet they remained standing outside the tower, unsure of what to do next. They'd been successful and solved the problem of the horrible warlock. Maybe they hadn't solved it in the way that any of them had expected, or even desired, but Grimgrax's reign of terror was finally over. Yet instead of cheering the outcome or congratulating each other, they did nothing.

Eventually Rev cleared her throat. "You know, after all we've been through, I'd say that we deserve a drink. How about it?"

There was a pause, and then the others began to nod in agreement.

"Great! I know a really good tavern close to here…"

THE LAST CHAPTER

The musician's instruments could barely be heard over the chattering voices within the tavern. They were in a small town called Humville, and yet the local tavern looked almost exactly like the one back in Quarryville, including the smirking barkeep and dirt-smeared locals.

The group had found a table in the back corner, hoping that it would be a relatively quiet place to celebrate, yet it was impossible to escape the towns-people's mirth, no matter how little they wanted to be a part of it.

Aeris noticed that Grendel and Rev had no problem tossing back their mugs of ale and going back to the bar for more, while Corin and she were slower drinkers, still on their first mug.

As she took a small sip of her ale, she couldn't help

marvelling at where she was and who she was with. The fact that they had all converged on that one town with similar intentions, fought against each other so hard, and yet still managed to work together as a team was incredible. Sure they'd gotten off to a shaky start, but in Grimgrax's tower they had been an actual group, each person looking out for and helping each other. She was going to miss it.

"I still can't believe you made me destroy the staff," Rev complained, finishing off her second ale.

"It was for the best," Corin spoke up, taking a small sip from his mug. "It was filled with dark magic, and if it had fallen into the wrong hands it could be disastrous."

"But think of how much money I could have sold it for..." She had taken other items on their way out of the tower, but nothing was as valuable as the staff.

"I still don't know if we did the right thing using those spells," Grendel muttered. "But at least he won't be hurting anyone anymore."

"And if you think about him as a doddering old man, stocking shelves behind a counter and getting yelled at by impatient customers, it's quite an amusing punishment," Rev chuckled.

Grendel's mouth quirked into a smile and the two of them shared a laugh.

"We did a really good job," Aeris said earnestly. "Not only did we manage to help a lot of people, but we were able to work as a team."

"Some people might call that a miracle," Corin laughed. When nobody else joined in, his face quickly fell. "I mean..."

"Don't worry," Aeris said gently. "After what happened during our first fight, I never would have thought that we'd be able to do something like that."

Rev upended her mug, trying to drain every last drop of ale from it. "So, what's everyone's plan for the future?"

Aeris didn't have to think about it. "Find more people to help and continue my paladin training."

Corin shrugged. "Maybe go back to the town. Try to work in a library?"

Grendel quietly stared at his mug.

Aeris wanted to give Grendel a few suggestions, but she wasn't sure if it was her place. He'd thought about revenge for so long, ignoring everything else in his life, and now he probably felt like a ship adrift in open waters. She was confident that he would find his way in the world sooner or later – he simply needed to be open to new opportunities.

"Well, I can't wait to get back to..." Rev paused. "...Helping people. Because that's what I do."

Corin burst out laughing and this time Rev joined him. Aeris shook her head, but she couldn't help smiling.

"Hey, are you the folks who defeated the evil warlock Grimgrax?"

They all turned to see a short, bearded man standing next to their table.

"Um, yes," Aeris replied. "May I ask how you know about that?" It had barely been two hours since Grimgrax's defeat and less than an hour since they'd set foot inside The Last Chapter for their victory drinks. How fast did word travel around these parts?

"Oh, I heard this one bragging about it at the bar," he pointed at Rev.

She didn't look the slighted bit ashamed. "We did a great thing and people deserve to know."

"I was wondering if you were free to take on another task," the man continued. "See, there's a cave of goblins near the edge of my farm, and they've been stealing my crops and damaging property. I was hoping you could help."

The four exchanged a look. At first, everyone was uncertain. Take on another task? As a group? But they weren't actually a group – they were merely four people who'd been thrown together in a crazy situation.

But Corin, Grendel, and Rev didn't seem to have any plans, and Aeris had said that she'd wanted to help people... And this man needed help...

Around the table, numerous expressions were exchanged, but soon all four were in agreement.

"We'd love to help," Aeris said brightly. "Where's your farm located?"

"How long do you think this will take?" Grendel asked.

"Just how many goblins are we talking about?" Corin added nervously.

"Do you want the usual rate or our deluxe package?" Rev smiled.

The man was taken aback by their sudden enthusiasm, and as he quickly tried to fill them in, Aeris couldn't help wondering what this next adventure would bring.

ABOUT THE AUTHOR

(Photo by Morgana Kay)

Ali is the author of sci-fi/fantasy novels *The Six Elemental* and *The Fifth Queen*, and the short story collection *The Lightbulb Forest*. Numerous short stories of hers have appeared in Engen Book's 'From the Rock' series.

She spends most of her time scribbling stories and ideas in notebooks, and is rarely found without paper and pen. She is an avid traveller, foodie, and fan of the Oxford comma.

Currently she lives in Halifax with her computer and four swords, surrounded by over-flowing book-shelves and too many ideas.

The early years of **Xander Drew** as he struggles with the evils of his small rural hometown of Coral Beach, Maine. Cursed with the heart of the Womb and the gift of seeing the world around him for what it really is, Xander must learn hard lessons about the nature of humanity to traverse the minefield of criminals, gangs, and abusers that stand between him and ultimate happiness

-- but most of all that **sometimes it takes a monster, to catch a monster.**

"THE WRITING OF ITS GENERATION- - VISUAL, TO-THE-POINT AND IN-THE-MOMENT."
- The Northeast Avalon Times

The Coral Beach Casefiles series by Matthew LeDrew:
Book One: Black Womb (February 2019)
Book Two: Transformations in Pain (March 2019)
Book Three: Smoke and Mirrors (April 2019)
Book Four: Roulette (May 2019)
Book Five: Ghosts of the Past (June 2019)
Book Six: Ignorance is Bliss (July 2019)
Book Seven: Becoming (August 2019)
Book Eight: Inner Child (September 2019)
Book Nine: Gang War (October 2019)
Book Ten: Chains (November 2019)
Epilogue: The Long Road (December 2019)

For more information, please visit
www.engenbooks.com